The Berenstain Bears
Go to School

When summertime ends
and the weather turns cool,
most little bears
are ready for school....

A Random House PICTUREBACK®

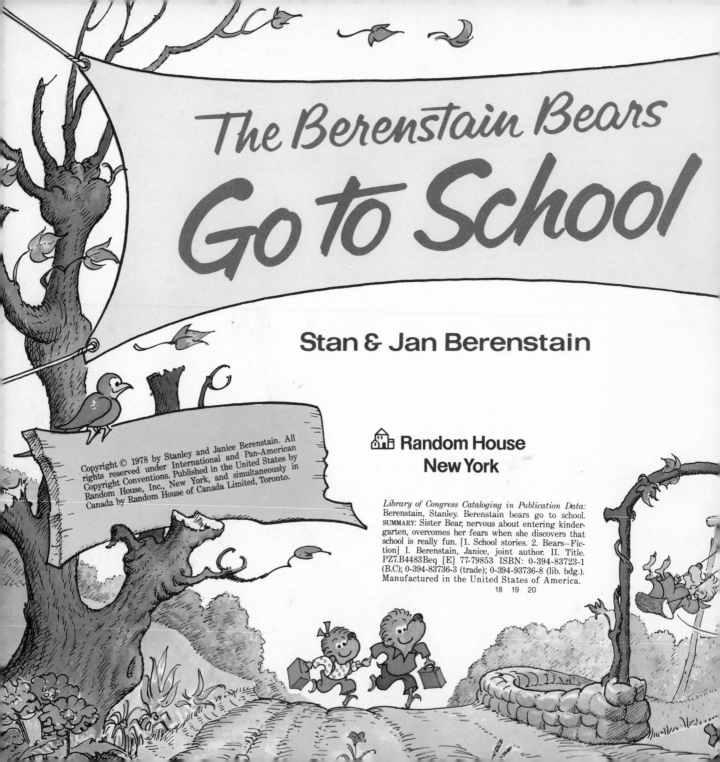

The Berenstain Bears
Go to School

Stan & Jan Berenstain

🏠 **Random House
New York**

Library of Congress Cataloging in Publication Data:
Berenstain, Stanley. Berenstain bears go to school.
SUMMARY: Sister Bear, nervous about entering kindergarten, overcomes her fears when she discovers that school is really fun. [1. School stories. 2. Bears—Fiction] I. Berenstain, Janice, joint author. II. Title.
PZ7.B4483Beq [E] 77-79853 ISBN: 0-394-83723-1 (B.C); 0-394-83736-3 (trade); 0-394-93736-8 (lib. bdg.).
Manufactured in the United States of America.
18   19   20

It had been a wonderful summer for the Bear family. They had gone swimming and boating at the lake. They had picnicked in the woods, and taken many walks along sunny paths.

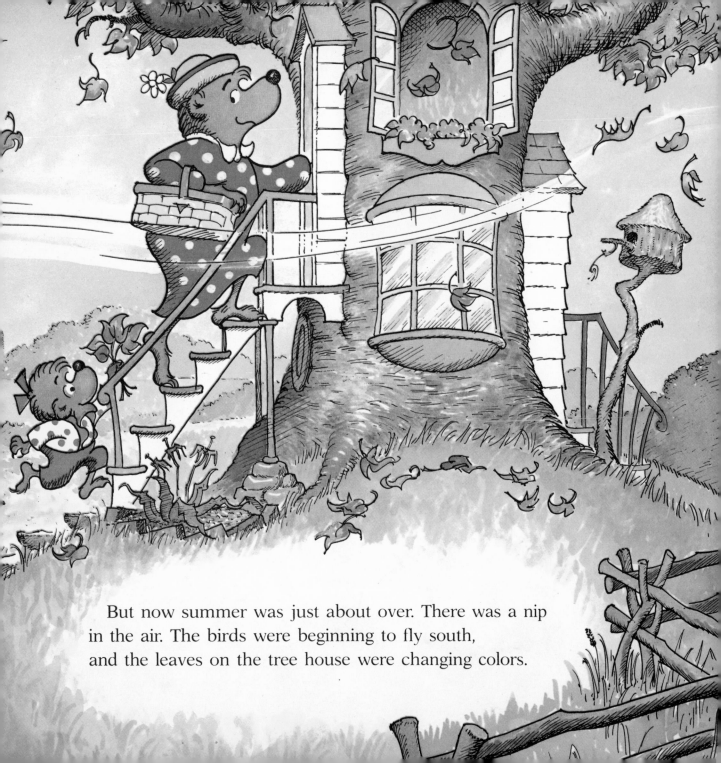

But now summer was just about over. There was a nip
in the air. The birds were beginning to fly south,
and the leaves on the tree house were changing colors.

One evening at supper, Brother Bear said, "I'm getting tired of summer vacation. I think I'm ready to go back to school!"

"That *is* good news," said Papa Bear. "Because school will be starting again, very soon!"

Sister Bear's ears perked up at the word *school*.

Mama Bear noticed. "As a matter of fact," she said, "Sister and I are going to meet her new teacher tomorrow."

This year Sister would be starting kindergarten. And she wasn't quite sure how she felt about it.

She liked being at home
with her mother and father...

her books and toys...

and all her friends.

"What will school be like, Mama?" she asked
at bedtime.

"You'll find out tomorrow," said Mama as she
tucked Sister in and kissed her good-night.

The next day, Mama and Sister packed a lunch and took the long walk down the winding dirt road to the Bear Country School.

Handybear Gus was up on a ladder, fixing the roof.
"Hello!" said Mama. "This is Sister Bear.
She starts kindergarten next week."
"We'll be glad to have her," said Gus.
"Miss Honeybear is the kindergarten teacher.
You'll find her inside."

"Hello there!" said Miss Honeybear in a loud, jolly voice. "Come right in and look around!"

Sister thought Miss Honeybear's voice was a little scary. But she let Miss Honeybear take her hand and lead her into the kindergarten room.

What a big friendly room! It had yellow
curtains and tables and chairs that looked
just right for someone Sister's size.

"What do you *do* in kindergarten?"
Sister asked as they sat down for lunch.
"We read stories, sing songs, learn our
ABCs, paint pictures, play games, make things
out of clay, build with blocks—we do *lots*
of things!" said Miss Honeybear.

The little bear who sat
next to Sister began to look
worried, so she smiled
at him and held his hand.

At last the bus arrived. The Bear Country School looked very nice. Handybear Gus had fixed the roof, and painted the trim, and cut the grass.

And Miss Honeybear's kindergarten room looked beautiful. Everything was ready!

Before very long, the kindergartners got noisy! Two of them wanted to play with the same dump truck. Two others wanted to look at the same book. And a whole gang of them wanted to be first to play with the blocks. What a commotion!

Suddenly a loud, jolly voice called out: "STORY TIME!" Miss Honeybear was calling the class to the book corner. *That* quieted things down.

After the story, Sister tried
everything. She painted a picture...

helped build a block city...

made a giant clay doughnut...

and looked at the books.

She ate all of her bread and
honey at snack time. . .

and she fell asleep
at nap time.

When she climbed off the bus
with Brother at the end of the day,
Sister was the excited one.

"Mama! Papa! Look what I did
in school today!" she said, holding
up her painting.

A few days later, the weather turned warm again, as it sometimes does in early fall.

Brother was restless at breakfast. "I wish it was still summer vacation," he said, "so I wouldn't have to go to school today."

"Oh, come on, Brother Bear!" said Sister. "School is fun. Let's get going or we'll miss the bus!"

On the bus, all the bears were talking about the things they were going to do at school— soccer practice, science projects, music lessons—all kinds of things!

H-m-m, thought Brother. Sister Bear was right. School *is* fun!

And off they went in the big yellow bus
to the Bear Country School.